NURTURE

Maxine Kumin won the Pulitzer Prize in 1973 and was Consultant in Poetry to the Library of Congress in 1981–82. Born in Philadelphia, she was educated at Radcliffe College and now lives in New Hampshire. In addition to *Nurture*, she is the author of four novels, eight volumes of poetry, a collection of essays on country living, and a collection of short stories. She has taught at several universities, including Washington University, Brandeis, Columbia University, and Princeton.

NURTURE
POEMS

MAXINE KUMIN

PENGUIN BOOKS

PENGUIN BOOKS
Published by the Penguin Group
Viking Penguin, a division of Penguin Books USA Inc.
40 West 23rd Street, New York, New York 10010 U.S.A.
Penguin Books Ltd, 27 Wrights Lane,
London W8 5TZ, England
Penguin Books Australia Ltd, Ringwood,
Victoria, Australia
Penguin Books Canada Ltd, 2801 John Street,
Markham, Ontario, Canada L3R 1B4
Penguin Books (N.Z.) Ltd, 182–190 Wairau Road,
Auckland 10, New Zealand

Penguin Books Ltd, Registered Offices:
Harmondsworth, Middlesex, England

First published in the United States of America by
Viking Penguin, a division of Penguin Books USA Inc. 1989
Published in Penguin Books 1989

1 3 5 7 9 10 8 6 4 2

Page vii constitutes an extension of this copyright page.

LIBRARY OF CONGRESS CATALOGING IN PUBLICATION DATA
Kumin, Maxine, 1925–
Nurture: poems / Maxine Kumin.
p.   cm.—(The Penguin poets)
ISBN 0 14 058.619 9
I. Title.
PS3521.U638N87   1989b
811'.54—dc19   89–31129

Printed in the United States of America
Set in Goudy Old Style

ACKNOWLEDGMENTS

The selections in this book originally appeared in *The Amicus Journal*, *Country Journal*, *Cream City Review*, *Crosscurrents Anthology*, *Emrys Journal*, *The Feminist Press 1970–1985: A Birthday Book* published by The Feminist Press at the City University of New York, *Graham House Review*, *Harvard Magazine*, *Kunitz Festschrift* published by Sheep Meadow Press, *Michigan Quarterly Review*, *The Nation*, *The New York Times*, *The Ontario Review*, *Organic Gardening*, *Pacific Review*, and *Redstart*.

"In Warm Rooms, Before a Blue Light," "In the Park," and "A Game of Monopoly in Chavannes" first appeared in *The New Yorker* and "Nurture," "With the Caribou," "On Reading an Old Baedeker in Schloss Leopoldskron," "The Festung, Salzburg," "Night Launch," " 'Primitivism' Exhibit," "Marianne, My Mother, and Me," and "A Calling" in *Poetry*.

CONTENTS

III   MORE TRIBAL POEMS

NURTURE

CATCHMENT

NURTURE

From a documentary on marsupials I learn
that a pillowcase makes a fine
substitute pouch for an orphaned kangaroo.

I am drawn to such dramas of animal rescue.
They are warm in the throat. I suffer, the critic proclaims,
from an overabundance of maternal genes.

Bring me your fallen fledgling, your bummer lamb,
lead the abused, the starvelings, into my barn.
Advise the hunted deer to leap into my corn.

And had there been a wild child—
filthy and fierce as a ferret, he is called
in one nineteenth-century account—

a wild child to love, it is safe to assume,
given my fireside inked with paw prints,
there would have been room.

Think of the language we two, same and not-same,
might have constructed from sign,
scratch, grimace, grunt, vowel:

Laughter our first noun, and our long verb, howl.

WITH THE CARIBOU

At the top of the world I want to go for a drive
in a primitive troika lightly harnessed to reindeer.
Behind three clove-brown creatures, yoked together
yet bridleless, guided only by a long pole
that the driver taps to indicate gee and haw
I want to sled over the alpine tundra
race through boreal forests of birch and aspen
and glide past the boggy taiga daggered with black spruce trees.

I want to leap up at the three-nation caribou parley
in Whitehorse, Yukon, to warn them the radionuclides
absorbed from the lichen they live on may kill them
if they don't drown in droves at crossings flooded
out by hydroelectric stations, or slowly
starve to death behind oil pipelines that posit
behavioral barriers they dare not soar over
or burst their aortas trying. I want to advise the species
to set up new herds, to mingle and multiply,

else how can I hurtle with them across the Kobuk River
at Onion Portage, be caught up in the streaming southward,
the harsh crowding of antlers uplifted like thousands
of stump-fingered arms? I'm slithering backward in time to
the Bering land bridge, awash at high tide, I cross over
nibbling down to Nevada, down to New Jersey,
I rejoice to be circumpolar, all of us
on all fours obeying the laws of migration.

IN WARM ROOMS, BEFORE A BLUE LIGHT

All over America tonight,
the males mince past us
gravely tall as dwarves in "Snow White,"

single file, edged with pathos,
a comedy in frock coats played
out on Antarctic ice.

Each bird balances an egg
between his belly and the tops
of his feet, more or less snug

against freezing. Some will drop
as weeks pass and the bizarre parade
exacts its ritual upkeep.

Meanwhile the females swim
far and deep, fattening up
for the regurgitations to come.

The males on this nearly doomed march
lose one-third of their body weight
hitching the eggs along till they hatch,

and then, with nothing to feed the brood,
must vomit what little fluid
they can into those beseeching maws.

Now the macabre dance begins
in the teeth of the polar wind.
It's sheer motion to stay alive:

Starved fathers and unfledged youngsters
in a huddle of down and feathers
shuffle and weave a tight circle

from which some chicks will fall over
and freeze solid, their infant feet
sticking straight up, until the hard night

eases and the ice breaks loose
and waves of mothers rush back,
their blubbery bodies storehouses

of food for the desperate flock.
The males are released for a two-month binge
of Rabelaisian feasting

beyond the ice shelf, barely
enough time to make ready
for the next onslaught of natural

selection, a ten-month struggle
that keeps the species afloat
with purgings and gorgings.

And is there pleasure in it
this bad hand Nature dealt them?
With zoom lenses we look in,

look in and wonder
at what flesh does for them—
we, who are going under.

THOUGHTS ON SAVING THE MANATEE

Weighed down by its dense bones
the manatee swims so slowly
that algae have time to
colonize on its spine.
I know a woman who rode
one down the river gently
scraping with a clamshell
letting drift free a bushel
basket of diatoms and kelp.

At one time you could order
manatee steak in any
restaurant in Florida.
It was said to taste like veal.
My friend reported that hers
bubbled and squealed its pleasure
beneath her making it well
worth risking a five hundred
dollar fine for molesting
this cow-size endangered aquatic
mammal whose name derives from
the Carib word for breast.

And from the overlook
at Blue Spring, pendulous
disembodied breasts
are what I see dappling
the play of sunlight on
the lagoon. They swim up here
from the St. Johns River

—mostly cows and their calves—
to disport in the temperate water

and stay to choke on
our discards. They swallow
snarls of fishing line or
the plastic ribbons that tie
beer cans together.
Along with acorns sucked
from the river bottom
they also ingest large numbers
of metal pop tops that razor

their insides. Grazing
on water hyacinths, they're
sideswiped by boat propellers.
Many have bled with bright scars
they come to be known by
and yet, many deaths
are mysterious, if not willful.
Worldwide less than five
thousand manatees remain.

For a small sum you can adopt one
through the Audubons.
Already named Boomer or Jojo
tricked out with a radio collar
it will ascend tranquilized
to be weighed and measured on schedule
but experts agree that no matter
how tenderly tamed by philanthropy
survival is chancy.

Consider my plan.
It's quick and humane:

Let's revert to the Catch of the Day
and serve up the last few as steak marinara.
Let's stop pretending we need them
more than they need us.

REPENT

A visual delight,
the killer whale.
Two-tone black and white
from snout to tail.
Worth hunting deep at sea.

And when we've captured two or three
we pen them in a little jail
and teach them tricks
to do for fishy snacks
for paying multitudes who fill

the stands and scream to see
these mammals leap in synchrony,
who cruise a hundred miles a day
when free
beneath the bounding main.

Occasionally from the strain
they turn upon the rubber-suited crew
who labor so to train
them to cavort on cue,
and even maim a few.

Stu-
pidity, said
Immanuel Kant,
is caused by a wicked
heart. Repent.

HOMAGE TO BINSEY POPLARS

O if we but knew what we do
When we delve or hew—
G. M. Hopkins

The arctic fox of Kiska now is quelled
not spared, not one that preyed upon the goose
the rare Aleutian goose, all, all are felled—

our only white fox (in the winter phase)
swept from the island for the goose's sake
by poison pellets scattered on the ice—

the small endangered goose around whose neck
a narrow ring of white may grow no more
unless the purge of foxes lures it back.

The fox that Russian traders brought ashore
in 1836 to multiply
thence to be harvested year after year

hung leanly on in Kiska till the sly
and fecund Norway rat with nearly nak-
ed tail arrived, shipborne by the Allies.

The rat that fed on garbage stayed to suck
the yolks from eggs, untidy omnivore.
Fox banqueted on goose but kept in check·

the Old World rat that bids now to devour
each wished-for clutch on Kiska, to the rue
of federal Fish and Wildlife officers

who, sizing up the prospects of the few
in saving one, eradicated two.

CUSTODIAN

Every spring when the ice goes out
black commas come scribbling across the shallows.
Soon they sprout forelegs.
Slowly they absorb their tails
and by mid-June, full-voiced, announce themselves.

Enter our spotted dog.
Every summer, tense with the scent of them,
tail arced like a pointer's but wagging
in anticipation, he stalks his frogs
two hundred yards clockwise around
the perimeter of this mucky pond,
then counterclockwise, an old pensioner
happy in his work.

Once every ten or so pounces
he succeeds, carries his captive north
in his soft mouth, uncorks him on the grass,
and then sits, head cocked, watching the slightly
dazed amphibian hop back to sanctuary.

Over the years the pond's inhabitants
seem to have grown accustomed
to this ritual of capture and release.
They ride untroubled in the wet pocket
of the dog's mouth, disembark in the meadow
like hitchhikers, and strike out again for home.

I have seen others of his species kill
and swallow their catch and then be seized
with violent retchings. I have seen children

corner polliwogs in the sun-flecked hollow
by the green rock and lovingly squeeze
the life out of them in their small fists.
I have seen the great blue heron swoop in
time after wing-slapping time to carry
frogs back to the fledglings in the rookery.

Nothing is to be said here
of need or desire. No moral arises
nor is this, probably, purgatory.
We have this old dog,
custodian of an ancient race of frogs,
doing what he knows how to do
and we too, taking and letting go,
that same story.

BRINGING BACK THE TRUMPETER SWAN

Sloughs of its down once fell to the prairie, like snow
as it chalked the bright skies of the North Temperate Zone.
Its range was as broad as the roving caribou
and the clack of its wings, as enormous flocks rose up
from trumpeter swan-favored muskegs and swamps,
startled the ear, like the smack of endless home runs.

It didn't take long to endanger the trumpeter swan.
By 1877 the Hudson Bay
Company had sold seventeen thousand skins
mostly for millinery use,
down covers, quill pens, powder puffs
and sundry Victorian *objets*.

In the wild its head and neck are often rust-red
from feeding in ferrous waters. There is
a salmon or flesh-colored stripe, like a fine cord,
at the base of the bill. This is called the grin line.
The voice of the trumpeter swan recalls the klaxon
that used to blare from the perilous taxis of Paris.

The mute swan makes an acceptable foster mother
for the now almost extinct trumpeter swan.
Eggs removed from a captive pair of the latter,
cradled against any possible crush or lurch,
were flown to a sequestered Great Lakes marsh
and inserted into a mute swan's nest, just when

they were thought to be two or three days from date of hatch.
Cygnets first cheep in the shell to establish a bond
with the broody above—essential with this batch.

Don't ask what became of the mute swan's eggs. Don't inquire
about the four hundred snapping turtles speared
from the marsh in advance of the trumpeter swan's

styrofoam-swaddled eggs. Snappers are not
on the endangered list. Never mind—
they're expendable too, the eggs of the mute.
Culling and killing this way, we are bound
to bring back from the brink the trumpeter swan
in the names of Charles Darwin and John James Audubon.

THE ACCOLADE OF THE ANIMALS

All those he never ate
appeared to Bernard Shaw
single file in his funeral
procession as he lay abed
with a cracked infected bone
from falling off his bicycle.
They stretched from Hampton Court
downstream to Piccadilly
against George Bernard's pillow
paying homage to the flesh
of man unfleshed by carnage.

Just shy of a hundred years
of pullets, laying hens
no longer laying, ducks, turkeys,
pigs and piglets, old milk cows,
anemic vealers, grain-fed steer,
the annual Easter lambkin,
the All Hallows' mutton,
ring-necked pheasant, deer,
bags of hare unsnared,
rosy trout and turgid carp
tail-walking like a sketch by Tenniel.

What a cortege it was:
the smell of hay in his nose,
the pungencies of the barn,
the courtyard cobbles slicked
with wet. How we omnivores
suffer by comparison
in the jail of our desires

17

salivating at the smell of char
who will not live on fruits
and greens and grains alone
so long a life, so sprightly, so cocksure.

NOTED IN *THE NEW YORK TIMES*

Lake Buena Vista, Florida, June 16, 1987

Death claimed the last pure dusky seaside sparrow
today, whose coastal range was narrow,
as narrow as its two-part buzzy song.
From hummocks lost to Cape Canaveral
this mouselike skulker in the matted grass,
a six-inch bird, plain brown, once thousands strong,
sang *toodle-raeeee azhee*, ending on a trill
before the air gave way to rocket blasts.

It laid its dull white eggs (brown specked) in small
neat cups of grass on plots of pickleweed,
bulrushes, or salt hay. It dined
on caterpillars, beetles, ticks, the seeds
of sedges. Unremarkable
the life it led with others of its kind.

Tomorrow we can put it on a stamp,
a first-day cover with Key Largo rat,
Schaus swallowtail, Florida swamp
crocodile, and fading cotton mouse.
How simply symbols replace habitat!
The tower frames at Aerospace
quiver in the flush of another shot
where, once indigenous, the dusky sparrow
soared trilling twenty feet above its burrow.

SLEEPING WITH ANIMALS

Nightly I choose to keep this covenant
with a wheezing broodmare who, ten days past due,
grunts in her sleep in the vocables
of the vastly pregnant. She lies down
on sawdust of white pine, its turp smell blending
with the rich scent of ammonia and manure.
I in my mummy bag just outside her stall
observe the silence, louder than the catch
in her breathing, observe gradations of
the ancient noneditorial dark; against
the open doorway looking south, observe
the paddock posts become a chain gang, each
one shackled leg and wrist; the pasture wall
a graveyard of bones that ground fog lifts and swirls.

Sleeping with animals,
loving my animals too much,
letting them run like a perfectly detached
statement by Mozart through all the other lines
of my life, a handsome family of serene
horses glistening in their thoughtlessness,
fear ghosts me still for my two skeletons:
one stillborn foal eight years ago.
One, hours old, dead of a broken spine.
Five others swam like divers into air,
dropped on clean straw, were whinnied to, tongued dry,
and staggered, stagey drunkards, to their feet,
nipped and nudged by their mothers to the teat.

Restless, dozy, between occasional coughs
the mare takes note of me and nickers. Heaves

herself up, explores the corners of
her feed tub. Sleeps a little, leg joints locked.
I shine my light across the bar to watch
the immense contours of her flanks rise and fall.
Each double-inhale is threaded to the life
that still holds back in its safe sac.
What we say to each other in the cold black
of April, conveyed in a wordless yet perfect
language of touch and tremor, connects
us most surely to the wet cave we all
once burst from gasping, naked or furred,
into our separate species.

Everywhere on this planet, birth.
Everywhere, curled in the amnion,
an unborn wonder.
Together we wait for this still-clenched burden.

ENCOUNTER IN AUGUST

Black bears are not particularly interested in flesh . . .
they have been seen in the fields eating string beans.
John McPhee

Inside the tepee that admits
sunlight to the underpart
he stands eating my Kentucky Wonders.
Downs pod after pod, spilling the beans,
the ones I'd saved for shelling out
this winter, thinking *soup*
when he'd gone deep, denned up.

This is not Eden, which ran
unfenced and was not intercropped,
Eden, where frost never overtook a patch.
We stand ten yards apart, two omnivores
not much interested in flesh.
I think he ought to smell me through his greed
or hear my heart outbeat his steady chomp

but nothing interrupts his lunch.
At last he goes the way the skunk
does, supreme egoist, ambling
into the woodlot on all fours
leaving my trellis flat and beanless
and yet I find the trade-off fair:
beans and more beans for this hour of bear.

CATCHMENT

When the she-leopard stalks and pounces on
an infant antelope, which one
am I rooting for? The newborn

I saw slip, moments ago, free
from the birth canal, struggle to its feet,
stagger against its mother's teat

and begin to nurse, both nervously
twitching tail stubs in the heat
and flies of the equator

or the big cat, in whose camouflaged lair
three helpless youngsters wait
so starved for meat that she dares

venture out to hunt by daylight?
I watch this living-color film unfold
with a friend, whose English bull

mastiff pup—as if
New Hampshire were the veldt, as if
its life depended on the chase—

leapt up last month to snatch
a newborn doe kid from her arms
and snapped its neck with one good shake.

Later, watching the after-afterglow
flush the whole sky pink, then darken,
we can almost discuss it, good and harm.

Nature a catchment of sorrows.
We hug each other. No lesson drawn.

PLACE NAMES AND DATELINES

ON READING AN OLD BAEDEKER
IN SCHLOSS LEOPOLDSKRON

Salzburg, Austria

Soft as beetpulp, the cover
of this ancient Baedeker.
The gold print has scabbed off the leather
but thirty-three tissue paper maps extend
from Vienna to Bosnia. One
of my grandfathers is in here somewhere
living in three rooms over his tailor
shop on the Judengasse in Salzburg or
Prague, stitching up frockcoats on Jew
Alley in Pilsen, or in the mews
of Vienna's Old Quarter,
my mother's loyal obsequious *Opa*
tugging his forelock whenever
the name of Franz Joseph is spoken.

In this edition you can still travel
by diligence down from Bad Ischl
to Hallstatt, where grottoes full of bones
of early Celt miners have been uncovered.
Whole families journey to see them
cycling single file, observing the caution
to keep to the left "because in
whatever part of the Empire you meet them,
troops on the march, sized by height
and moving smartly, always keep right."

Not for you, *Opa*, this tourist attraction,
punts lapping the stone-green lake in
the hanging valley of Hallstatt,

languorous voices hovering
adrift in dappled sunlight
and the Lionel-toy train tunneling
out of its papier-mâché mountain
to pause at the cardboard station
where day trippers, disembarking,
may visit the fake antique ruin,
a mossed-over stucco *folly*.
Time to shoulder your knapsack
and strike out for Ellis Island.
Kiss your nine sisters and never look back.

Never look back, Grandfather.
Don't catch my eye on this marble
staircase as wide as the 'gasse
you lived in. Don't look at the chandeliers
that shone on the Nazi Gauleiter
who moved in and made this headquarters.
Here in the cavernous Great Hall
I look for some thin line of comfort
that binds us, some weight-bearing bridge

and finally walk out in rain
to fling stale rolls to the swans
in their ninetieth generation.

THE FESTUNG, SALZBURG

I shall have to pee out the window, says the translation
in the 1902 pocket phrasebook Alastair's
grandfather gave him. Also, *Call the hostler!*
and *Here are my boots,* meaning polish them
but nothing that helps decipher life in this fortress
four hundred years ago, all cobble and cannon,
all ice storms and armor and horses. How, for example,
did they haul water for livestock and people?
Out of what reservoir make time for
carving twelve marble apostles and a Christ
that are tucked in a chapel chipped from the rock
of the scarp that commands the Salzach?
No idiom to tell us how secure
this Festung was before war took the air.

Down in the candybox town we dawdle
at Tomaselli's over cups of hot chocolate.
I pretend I have come back here for the sake
of my forebears, come back out of exile
to reinvent how it was for them,
seeking among the faces that pass
those as old as I, those few with missing
limbs, or sightless, who endured the Anschluss,
seeking among the dirndls and lederhosen
the unknowable middleaged ones who risked the ovens
and came through stained with a deep understanding.
Bitte, bitte schön. Ropes of rain
fall on a sea of purposeful umbrellas
in calm green homogeneous Austria.

NIGHT LAUNCH

Canaveral Seashore National Park

Full moon. Everyone in silhouette
graying just this side of color as we wait:
babies in Snuglis, toddlers from whose clutches
ancient blankets depend, adults encumbered
with necklaces of cameras, binoculars.
A city of people gathered on the beach.
Expectant boats jockeying offshore.

When we were kids we used to race
reciting *the seething sea ceaseth;*
thus the sea sufficeth us
and then collapse with laughter, never
having seen the rise-and-fall of ocean,
the lip of foam like seven-minute icing,
moon-pricked dots of plankton skittering.

The horizon opens, floods with daybreak,
a rosy sunrise as out of sync
as those you fly into crossing the Atlantic,
midnight behind you, the bald sky blank,
and up comes the shuttle, one costly Roman candle,
orange, silent, trailing as its rockets fall
away a complicated snake of vapor.

Along the beach a feeble cheer.
Muffled thumps of blastoff, long after,
roll like funeral drums, precise and grave.
We are the last to leave.
Driving back along the asphalt, signed
every hundred yards "Evacuation Route"
past honeycombs of concrete condominiums

I remember how we wrapped and carried
our children out to a suburban backyard
to see Sputnik cross the North Temperate Zone
at two in the morning, and how we shivered
watching that unwinking little light
move east without apparent cause.
On this warm seacoast tonight
in the false dawn my neckhairs rose.
Danger flew up to uncertain small applause.

"PRIMITIVISM" EXHIBIT

Museum of Modern Art, 1984

In spite of admonitions not
to loose my psyche in this primal landscape
I get off on the wrong foot
misread Ibibio as libido
then must duck so as not to scrape
the Soul-catcher's noose of hanging O's.

Worse, there's God A'a, whose maggoty people
I take as a lesson in fleshcreep.
At the site of umbilicus, nipples
eyes, ears, nose, chin
hips and kneecaps
cling clay Lilliputians

upside down and sideways.
Leeches fasten like this in stagnant ponds
but nobody knows what the statue meant to say.
Maybe it was a frozen happening,
an art event on Rurutu Island.
Maybe a second, or 32nd, coming.

Longest I look at the dread
dog fetish, whose spiky back
is built of rusty razorblades
that World War II GI's let drop
on atolls in the South Pacific
they were securing from the Japs

who did not shave, but only plucked
stray hairs from chin and jowl.
I like the way he makes a funk-
y art out of cosmetic junk
standing the cutting edge of old steel
up straight to say, *World, get off my back.*

PHOTOGRAPH, MARYLAND AGRICULTURAL COLLEGE LIVESTOCK SHOW, 1924

Blond, wholesome, serene,
their white shirtsleeves rolled,
these boys in white ducks
keep sleek black hogs at their feet,
hogs cleaner than licorice sticks in the sun.
Five haltered calves are also held
in tandem while their names
and pedigrees are said aloud.

Mostly I think about
the unseen mud and manure, flies
and screwworms that connect these boys
and their wildest hopes
poised radiant between two wars
while just out of reach of the lens
in their stained bib overalls
stand the farm laborers

greasy with sweat
and undoubtedly black.

PHOTOGRAPH, U.S. ARMY FLYING SCHOOL, COLLEGE PARK, MARYLAND, 1909

Wilbur Wright is racing the locomotive
on the Baltimore and Ohio commuter line.
The great iron horse hisses and hums on its rails
but the frail dragonfly overhead appears to be winning.
Soon we will have dog fights and the Red Baron.
The firebombing of Dresden is still to come.
And the first two A-bombs, all that there are.

The afterburners of jets lie far in the future
and the seeds of our last descendants, who knows,
are they not yet stored in their pouches?

ON BEING ASKED TO WRITE A POEM
IN MEMORY OF ANNE SEXTON

The elk discards his antlers every spring.
They rebud, they grow, they are growing

an inch a day to form a rococo rack
with a five-foot spread even as we speak:

cartilage at first, covered with velvet;
bendable, tender gristle, yet

destined to ossify, the velvet sloughed off,
hanging in tatters from alders and scrub growth.

No matter how hardened it seems there was pain.
Blood on the snow from rubbing, rubbing, rubbing.

What a heavy candelabrum to be borne
forth, each year more elaborately turned:

the special issues, the prizes in her name.
Above the mantel the late elk's antlers gleam.

IN THE PARK

You have forty-nine days between
death and rebirth if you're a Buddhist.
Even the smallest soul could swim
the English Channel in that time
or climb, like a ten-month-old child,
every step of the Washington Monument
to travel across, up, down, over or through
—you won't know till you get there which to do.

He laid on me for a few seconds
said Roscoe Black, who lived to tell
about his skirmish with a grizzly bear
in Glacier Park. *He laid on me*
not doing anything. I could feel
his heart beating against my heart.
Never mind *lie* and *lay*, the whole world
confuses them. For Roscoe Black you might say
all forty-nine days flew by.

I was raised on the Old Testament.
In it God talks to Moses, Noah,
Samuel, and they answer.
People confer with angels. Certain
animals converse with humans.
It's a simple world, full of crossovers.
Heaven's an airy Somewhere, and God
has a nasty temper when provoked,
but if there's a Hell, little is made of it.
No longtailed Devil, no eternal fire,

and no choosing what to come back as.
When the grizzly bear appears, he lies/lays down
on atheist and zealot. In the pitch-dark
each of us waits for him in Glacier Park.

PART III

MORE
TRIBAL
POEMS

MARIANNE, MY MOTHER, AND ME

I close the book I am reading in which
there's a picnic in the country before the Great War.
William Carlos Williams has motored over
from Rutherford and lots of the Greenwich
Village crowd come up with cheese and bread
and Marianne Moore arrives with her bright red hair
in braids wound twice around her head,

as long as that. She's the same age as my mother,
who deftly plays four hands at the piano
in the Conservatory and flirts so
outrageously she has to elope with my father.
At this picnic, Alfred Kreymborg—it's his place—
hands around the stuffed eggs and everyone
sits on the ground in attitudes of such grace
that tears come into my eyes for what is gone,

for the intensity of it, I think I mean,
the way the poets turn up in each other's
richly detailed literary memoirs
making the dangerous era we live in seem
pallid, empty at least of artistic passion.
That same year my father buys a Stanley Steamer.
He and my mother wheel past, the toast of the town
in their matching linen dusters and gay demeanor,

but this perfect picture is flawed with spider cracks.
His only brother is soon to be gassed at the Marne.
My housebound mother, crazed with her first-born,
opens the lid of the Steinway with an axe.

Nevertheless, the next babe and the next and next
come forth in jig time, though Pa, ascending
among the nouveaux riches on Wall Street specs,
is seldom home. Released from baby-tending

by a starchy Nanny, Momma finds renown
as a demon shopper. Chopin is packed away.
A wet bar flows in the space of the vanquished Steinway
and obsequious salesladies all over town
call up to describe designer frocks on sale.
Meanwhile, Marianne's father, in despair
over his failure to provide the wherewithal
for his family, blinks twice and disappears.

Our heroine, undaunted, graduates
from Bryn Mawr and teaches stenography
in an American Indian school upstate,
becomes a librarian, an editor, and inch
by inch the closet poet emerges. "We
must be as clear as our natural reticence
will allow," she announces. Rapturously

I try this statement on like a negligee
that's neither diaphanous nor yet opaque.
Crisp lyrics from her quirky intellect
flare across Modern Poetry Survey
where she's sandwiched between Pound and Ransom.
But not once in my four years as a Cliffie,
humble in Harvard Yard, do I find that phantom
I long for, a woman professor, trailed by her covey.

Pearl Harbor bursts apart. Cambridge fills
with uniforms. How to accommodate

the life of the mind with the inmost patriot?
Six days a week at dawn in Sever Hall
toward that end, I take intensive Russian
with crewcut p.f.c.'s quickmarched from barracks.
My mother attends air raid warden sessions.
Marianne writes "In Distrust of Merits":

Strengthened to live, strengthened to die, for medals . . .
My brothers ship out, each to a different theater.
Sunlight glints on the B School's 90-day wonders,
those all-boy ensigns. I try for the WACs but am stalled.
Hiroshima melts down. Sweet peace, reprieve.
Marianne embarks on La Fontaine.
I graduate, get married; *too young,* Mother weeps,
and yet we're liver-spotted with dead friends.

Soon after, my mother's a volunteer. She reads
to the blind, pricks Beethoven in braille, makes
weekly side trips to the Philharmonic
and suddenly it's the fifties. I've become
a freshman English instructor, a freshman poet
as well. Marianne is reading her poems
at Wellesley. Surely the ones I know by heart

will trickle through the leaky microphone.
My fingers riffle pages of the texts
but the black tricorn bending low deflects
that flat small voice from reaching anyone.
I tell myself, it's like Faulkner's "The Bear":
You must relinquish everything to enter
into its presence. Except that having come there
I'm eye to eye with what? An eccentric spinster

whom I can't emulate, however much
I admire her words that "cluster like chromosomes."
Strong emotion has no place in her poems
but slithers into every line I touch.
We never meet. I am content to take
to heart her praise of idiosyncrasy,
exactitude, intensity, technique.
Her "be accurate and modest" speaks to me.

When Robert Lowell puffs her as "the best
woman poet in English," I thrill to hear
Langston Hughes's riposte: "I consider her
[it's 1953] the most famous
Negro woman poet in America."
A vintage year—my third child is born.
From her grandmother bracelet, nine criteria
of my mother's worth dangle, each name a charm.

Here's Marianne posing for *Life* magazine
at the zoo. Here, rooting for the Brooklyn Dodgers.
Here, *The New Yorker* prints an exchange of letters
between the poet and the corporate machine
as Ford invites Miss Moore to find a name
for its disastrous Edsel. None of hers
would do, though fanciful and fleet of limb.
The sixties roll round. My first book appears.

This is the decade in which assassination
catches on, like a vile pop tune. We mourn
a president who was briefly everyone's darling.
We mourn his brother. Sexton and I in the rain
sway with thousands on Boston Common
to hear Martin Luther King. And then we lose him
and lose Evers and Schwerner, Cheney, and Goodman
and all of us lose heart in Vietnam.

Little from Marianne of praise or caveat
in these years. Reviewing a new anthology
she opens herself to report that Allen G.
"can foul the nest in a way to marvel at,"
but nothing she says impinges on events.
"Greed seems to me the vice of the century,"
she writes in *Seventeen*. On a Central Park bench
she poses with Mickey Spillane for an airline venture,

not for the fee from Braniff, but because it feels
impolite to her to refuse. My mother, I'm sure
would agree. I wonder, at that early *déjeuner sur
l'herbe,* can Marianne turn down the wassail?
Over the years each tries on rich disguises.
The poet becomes her beasts in armor and shell,
a woman adept at the wittiest camouflages
but under them always lurks the shy red-haired girl

while my mother pretends not to find old age bewildering.
Widowed, she takes up art. She goes on cruises.
Snapshots of the several great-grandchildren
accompany her. Though she hears less and less
she keeps her Friday seat at Symphony
and keeps the program notes, along with clips
of my reviews. Thus pass the seventies.
The end's in sight. First Marianne slips

away, original and last of her line.
Soon after, my mother, the dowager queen
leaving behind descendants like a string
of worry beads. I claim them both as mine
whose lives began in a gentler time and place
of horse-drawn manners, parlor decorum

—though no less stained with deception and regret—
before man split the atom, thrust the jet,
procured the laser, shot himself through space,
both shapers of my alphabet.

SURPRISES

This morning's red sun licks dew from the hundred
California peppers that never set fruit in
my Zone-Three garden. After fifteen summers

of failure why this year do I suffer
the glut of inordinate success? They hang
in clustered pairs like newly hatched sex organs.

Doubtless this means I am approaching
the victory of poetry over death
where art wins, chaos retreats, and beauty

albeit trampled under barbarism
rises again, shiny with roses, no thorns.
No earwigs, cutworms, leaf miners either.

Mother's roses climbed the same old latticework
trellis until it shattered under their weight
and she mourned the dirtied blossoms more, I thought,

than if they'd been her children. She pulled on
goatskin gloves to deal with her arrangements
in chamberpots, pitchers, and a silver urn.

I watched, orphan at the bakeshop window.
It took all morning. *Never mix species
or colors*, she lectured. *It cheapens them.*

At the end of her long life she could reel off
the names of all the cart horses that had
trundled through her childhood, and now that I

look backward longer than forward, nothing
too small to remember, nothing too slight
to stand in awe of, her every washday

Monday baked stuffed peppers come back to me
full of the leftovers she called surprises.

A CALLING

Over my desk Georgia O'Keeffe says
I have no theories to offer and then
takes refuge in the disembodied
third person singular: *One works*
I suppose because it is the most
interesting thing one knows to do.
O Georgia! Sashaying between
first base and shortstop as it were
drawing up a list of all the things
one imagines one has to do . . .
You get the garden planted. You
take the dog to the vet. You
certainly have to do the shopping.

Syntax, like sex, is intimate.
One doesn't lightly leap from person
to person. *The painting,* you said,
is like a thread that runs
through all the reasons for all the other
things that make one's life.
O awkward invisible third person,
come out, stand up, be heard!
Poetry is like farming. It's
a calling, it needs constancy,
the deep woods drumming of the grouse,
and long life, like Georgia's, who
is talking to one, talking to me,
talking to you.

TURNING THE GARDEN IN MIDDLE AGE

They have lain a long time, these two:
parsnip with his beard on his foot,
pudding stone with fool's gold in her ear
until, under the thrust of my fork,
earthlock lets go. Mineral
and marrow are flung loose in May
still clinging together as if
they had intended this embrace.

I think then of skulls picked clean
underground, and the long bones
of animals overturned in the woods
and the gorgeous insurgency
of these smart green weeds
erect now in every furrow
that lure me once more
to set seeds in the loam.

BRINGING THE LITTLE ONES BACK

Like twin skeins of tangled knitting yarn
the Scotch Highland heifers in the pasture
lie down under my bedroom window
to work their cuds. Between unblinking
ruminations they consume a glut
of poison ivy, burdock, blackberry thorns
and all deciduous leaves up to the browse line.
Their white mucilaginous muzzles
remind me how in grammar school I dipped
great globs of paste from the earthen pot
and stickered clumps of two-legged cows.

At night these moony yaks become ghosts
in my landscape. If one strays
from the other's side, each of the lost
utters a soft oceanic sob
like a foghorn lowing across the bay.
Wearing their dangerous horns like toys,
silent in blizzards, blackflies, and the spring
rain, they stay put like dolls at a tea party.
They are the Golliwogs, the Wouldbegoods,
orphans in all weathers come
back to make me better than I am.

REVIEWING THE SUMMER AND WINTER CALENDAR
OF THE NEXT LIFE

If death comes in July, they'll put me down
for barn swallow, consigned to an 18-hour
day of swoopings and regurgitations.
No sooner the first set of fledglings lined up
five perfect clones on the telephone wire
than another quartet of eggs erupts in the slap-
dab nest. *Is there no rest in this life?*
the parents beseech each time I forget
not to open the door under their house
attached to the porch stringers. Even the dog
slinks past when they dive, scolding, clearing the stage
for their juveniles finally flapping aloft.

If January, I'll get to pick and choose
among the evening grosbeaks bombing the feeder
in a savage display of yellow scapulars
or return as a wild turkey, one of the brace
who come at a waddle at 10 A.M.
punctual comics, across the manure pile
for their illicit fix of feedbin corn
or join the juncos, whose job description involves
sweeping up after everybody else,
even venturing in to dust the stalls
of the barn for stray or recycled specks of grain.

I only ask not ever to come back as
weasel, present but seldom seen in summer
darting from rock to hummock in his tacky fur.
Reptilian, equally slim of head and hip,
he can be caught sight of at ten below

stained dingy white in his unbleached muslin cape.
Rat-toothed egg-sucker, making do
like any desperate one of us, he slips
through the least crack into the food chain
chipping and chewing his way past links of rust
to claim our kingdom for his own.

GRAPPLING IN THE CENTRAL BLUE

Benevolent blue air
of October
I take you into custody
as I do the memories
of 1940 and before—
the unemployed uncles
hangdog in the yard
playing touch football
shooting squirrels
Elmer Davis and the bad news
crackling through Bakelite—
when we did not know
we were waiting for war.

I declare you
Month I Will Not Let Go Of
October
I take you into my arms
even as festoons
of mushrooms, adorned beneath
with accordion-pleated gills
attack the punky elms
and fasten on their decay.
Year after year
in one part of the woodland
they erupt from the bark
in elaborate layers.

Dropkicked the football
goes tacking
across the yard from

Oscar to Dan to Joe
the air full of their breathing
their roughneck calls
the ballet
of their ankles and elbows
those bad boys my father
despairs of ever unhousing
and their Cuba Libras
(his rum) safely behind
the clothesline goalposts.

One is to die by torpedo.
One in a swamp on maneuvres.
Only the oldest, at a great age
a child again, outlasts my father
to drift off alone in bed.
What awaits us
is hardly to be thought of.
Let us eat of the inland oyster.
Let its fragrance intoxicate us
into almost believing
that staying on is possible
again this year in
benevolent blue October.

MAGELLAN STREET, 1974

This is the year you fall in
love with the Bengali poet,
and the Armenian bakery stays open
Saturday nights until eleven
across the street from your sunny
apartment with steep fo'c'sle stairs
up to an attic bedroom.
Three-decker tenements flank you.
Cyclone fences enclose
flamingos on diaper-size lawns.

This is the year, in a kitchen
you brighten with pots of basil
and untidy mint, I see how
your life will open, will burst from
the maze in its walled-in garden
and streak toward the horizon.
Your pastel maps lie open
on the counter as we stand here
not quite up to exchanging
our lists of sorrows, our day books,
our night thoughts, and burn the first batch
of chocolate walnut cookies.

Of course you move on,
my circumnavigator.
Tonight as I cruise past your corner,
a light goes on in the window.
Two shapes sit at a table.

THE BANGKOK GONG

Home for a visit, you brought me
a circle of hammered brass
reworked from an engine part
into this curio
to be struck with a wad of cotton
pasted onto a stick.
Third World ingenuity
you said, reminds you
of Yankee thrift.

The tone of this gong
is gentle, haunting, but
hard struck three times
can call out as far
as the back fields
to say Supper
or, drummed darkly,
Blood everywhere!
Come quick.

When barely touched it imitates
the deep nicker the mare makes
swiveling her neck
watching the foal swim
out of her body.
She speaks to it even as
she pushes the hindlegs clear.
Come to me is her message
as they curl to reach each other.

Now that you are
back on the border

numbering the lucky ones
whose visas let them
leave everything behind
except nightmares, I hang
the gong on my doorpost.
Some days I
barely touch it.

WE STOOD THERE SINGING

On a gray day in March in his first year
we drove up out of orderly Geneva
mother and daughter and the daughter's child
up the hairpin turns of the Chasseral
in search of the horses of the Franches-Montagnes
with feathered fetlocks and manes blown wild
each splashed-white face the same, the same kind eye
said to persist unchanged since Charlemagne.

The baby slept tipped sideways in his chair
slept through sudden snow squalls that blanked
the alpine road like a stage scrim
and woke up cranky in Les Breûleux where
at the village's one store we stopped to take
our bearings. When he howled, the aproned woman
invited us back, past vats of sauerkraut
and wheels of cheese into their bedroom.

I remember that plain space of rough white plaster
oaken crucifix, oak beams overhead
runner of tatted lace on the chest of drawers.
I remember the lambskin she unrolled on the bed
motioning you to lay him down, and after
he was done up sweet with powder, she opened her arms
and bounced him chortling around the room
singing him bits of *le bon roi Dagobert*.

We stood there singing.
I remember
that moment of civility among women.

DISTANCE

What does it mean, I ask myself, while I am mowing
with the Tuff-Cut, slicing through a sprawl
of buttercups, graying pussytoes, and the unfurled
pale green tongues of milkweed in the pasture, how
do I, who buried both my parents long ago,
attach my name and number to another birthday?

Whoever mows with a big machine like this,
with two forward speeds and a wheel clutch, nippled hand grips,
a lever to engage the cutting blade, is androgynous
as is old age, especially for us marathoners.

We are growing into one sex, a little leathery
but loving, appreciating the air of midday
embroidered with leaping insects, the glint glancing from
the flanks of grazing horses, the long puppyhood of the young.

Around me old friends (and enemies) are beleaguered
with cancer or clogged arteries. I ought to be
melancholy inching upward through my sixties
surrounded by the ragged edges of so many acres,
parlaying the future with this aerobic mowing,
but I take courage from a big wind staving off the deerflies,

ruffling and parting the grasses like a cougar if there
were still cougars. I am thankful for what's left that's wild:
the coydogs who howl in unison when a distant fire siren
or the hoot owl starts them up, the moose that muddled
through the winter in the swampland behind us, the bears
that drop their spoor studded with cherry pits in our swales.

If I could free a hand behind this Tuff-Cut
I'd tug my forelock at the sow and her two cubs I met
at high noon last week on the trail to Bible Hill.
Androgyny. Another birthday. And all the while
the muted roar of satisfactory machinery.
May we flourish and keep our working distance.

A GAME OF MONOPOLY IN CHAVANNES

Each time I look up from the board to the rusty vineyards
I can see, through mist like grains of finest pollen
large dogs being walked, straining against their collars.

Higher up in the Jura, a light snow, *un peu timide*
they say here, sifts down on rounded humps of hills.
The chic white lacquered table we sit around,

three generations, smells of newness still.
It came in parts, like a child's intricate toy.
Assembling it was an hour's play . . . In my mind

I've landed on Boardwalk again and cannot pay,
the Bank is cheating me blind, it's the late thirties.
Too young to do sums, I am almost always in tears.

My brothers, two cousins and I, unaware
we are sent here each summer out of filial duty
squabble over St. James Place and the Short Line

in our grandmother's fusty Atlantic Avenue flat.
From Oma's front room overlooking the Boardwalk
we can hear the surf break and sigh sucking back

but we're unaware of the irony of place:
cheap haven for the Depression's pensioners.
To us Atlantic City is paradise

except when it rains like this, except when we hear
Oma's foreign words that speak pain and terror.
We buck up to decide whose turn to roll the dice

on the massive bleached oak table scrubbed with lemon
its six carved legs ending in jungly claws . . .
My grandson's in jail. He has failed three times

to throw releasing doubles. He has failed
to pass Go, lost two hundred dollars, and then
having paid his fine, lands on Luxury Tax.

His lower lip trembles, this luxury of a child
who burst naked into our lives, like luck.
Our sole inheritor, he has taken us over

with his oceanic wants, his several passports.
I will deed him the Reading Railroad, the Water Works,
the Electric Company, my hotel on Park Place.

All that I have is his, under separate cover
and we are the mortgaged nub of all that he has.
Soon enough he will learn, buying long, selling short

his ultimate task is to stay to usher us out.

FOR THE BEST IN PAPERBACKS, LOOK FOR THE

In every corner of the world, on every subject under the sun, Penguin represents quality and variety—the very best in publishing today.

For complete information about books available from Penguin—including Pelicans, Puffins, Peregrines, and Penguin Classics—and how to order them, write to us at the appropriate address below. Please note that for copyright reasons the selection of books varies from country to country.

In the United Kingdom: For a complete list of books available from Penguin in the U.K., please write to *Dept E.P., Penguin Books Ltd, Harmondsworth, Middlesex, UB7 0DA.*

In the United States: For a complete list of books available from Penguin in the U.S., please write to *Dept BA, Penguin*, Box 120, Bergenfield, New Jersey 07621-0120.

In Canada: For a complete list of books available from Penguin in Canada, please write to *Penguin Books Ltd, 2801 John Street, Markham, Ontario L3R 1B4.*

In Australia: For a complete list of books available from Penguin in Australia, please write to the *Marketing Department, Penguin Books Ltd, P.O. Box 257, Ringwood, Victoria 3134.*

In New Zealand: For a complete list of books available from Penguin in New Zealand, please write to the *Marketing Department, Penguin Books (NZ) Ltd, Private Bag, Takapuna, Auckland 9.*

In India: For a complete list of books available from Penguin, please write to *Penguin Overseas Ltd, 706 Eros Apartments, 56 Nehru Place, New Delhi, 110019.*

In Holland: For a complete list of books available from Penguin in Holland, please write to *Penguin Books Nederland B.V., Postbus 195, NL-1380AD Weesp, Netherlands.*

In Germany: For a complete list of books available from Penguin, please write to *Penguin Books Ltd, Friedrichstrasse 10-12, D-6000 Frankfurt Main 1, Federal Republic of Germany.*

In Spain: For a complete list of books available from Penguin in Spain, please write to *Longman, Penguin España, Calle San Nicolas 15, E-28013 Madrid, Spain.*

In Japan: For a complete list of books available from Penguin in Japan, please write to *Longman Penguin Japan Co Ltd, Yamaguchi Building, 2-12-9 Kanda Jimbocho, Chiyoda-Ku, Tokyo 101, Japan.*